The Unexpected Stranger

By

Lady Jay

Table of Contents

Dedication

- To God, the ultimate source of my strength, guidance, and peace.

- To my husband, whose unexpected impact has taught lessons of resilience, patience, and unexpected growth.

- To my late father and my mother, I thank you for your unconditional love, strength, and the wisdom you have imparted throughout my life.

- To my son, your love, strength, and relentless support have been my greatest source of inspiration.

- To my support system, my sisterhood - my girlfriends, close family, and my therapist, who stood by me and provided encouragement, understanding, and invaluable guidance, serving as my pillars of strength when I needed them the most.

Forwards

My friendship—or as I fondly call it, our "sistership"—with Lady Jay began through a simple introduction from her parents. What started as an introduction grew into a bond filled with trust, laughter, and a deep sense of support. Over the years, I have witnessed the immense compassion and strength she pours into every relationship. Her unwavering faith in God and genuine love for others have been like an anchor, not only in her life but also in mine. It's a blessing to have someone whose love and support help carry you through life's storms, and Lady Jay has been that person for me.

In *The Unexpected Stranger,* Lady Jay offers readers a heartfelt glimpse into her world, tackling the kinds of challenges many of us face but rarely talk about openly. Her aim is clear: she wants to empower others—especially women who may find themselves navigating tough, sometimes isolating, journeys. She speaks with candor about relationships, the ups and downs of mental health, and the unexpected moments that have shaped her. Through these reflections, she hopes to connect with readers who might also be struggling, encouraging them to embrace their own journeys and reminding them they're not alone.

Her words are more than just storytelling; they are laced with wisdom and insights born from real-life experiences. Within these pages, readers will find reassurance, hope, and the gentle reminder that even through disappointments, there's a light to follow. Life is filled with unexpected twists and turns, and Lady Jay doesn't shy away from sharing how she found courage and resilience amidst those moments. She offers her story as a beacon, showing that challenges can indeed lead us to a greater sense of purpose and strength.

One of the most inspiring aspects of Lady Jay's journey is her dedication to leaving a legacy. She writes with a deep awareness that her story is not just for herself but for the next generation—her family and loved ones. In sharing her thoughts and emotions so openly, she's creating a gift for them: a glimpse into her heart and the lessons she learned along the way. Through this, she reminds all of us of the importance of reflection and of finding meaning in our life stories.

I truly believe that *The Unexpected Stranger* is more than just a book; it's a testament to resilience, hope, and the power of vulnerability. Lady Jay invites us all to look within ourselves, to embrace our own struggles, and to find strength in community and faith. Her story encourages us to confront our fears, cherish our relationships, and build a legacy of love and courage. As you read this book, my hope is that you'll feel inspired to see your own life through a new lens—to recognize the beauty in each chapter and the strength in every challenge.

So, embark on this journey with Lady Jay. Let her words uplift you, her experiences guide you, and her faith inspire you. You may just find the courage to embrace the "unexpected strangers" in your life as well.

Sheila Edens-Brown, Certified VA/Coach

Marketing Strategist/Business Coach

The Unexpected Stranger is a journey in the life of Lady Jay, who I have known for 30 + years and who my husband, King Solomon Smallwood, a retired Pastor of the Seventh-day Adventist Church for 50 + years, and I have been a spiritual counselor in Lady Jay and her spouse's life. In our journey called life, we have encountered many unexpected strangers, including the one that lies within us! It is how we respond to and manage these strangers that aide in our physical, mental, and spiritual development, which ultimately is to bring honor and glory to God!

It is my prayer that as you read *The Unexpected Stranger* you will have an intimate knowledge of the author and her life, you will find gems that you can collect and place in your treasure chest, as keepsakes to aide in your life's journey, and to share with others. Afterall, the Bible reminds us that we are all God's children, and as brothers and sisters, we are to love and take care of one another, as Jesus Christ, our Brother, loves and takes "good" care of us!

Deborah L. Smallwood,

Manager Retiree of the U.S. Treasury Department, Clergy Spouse, and Praise and Worship Leader at the West End Seventh-day Adventist Church in Atlanta, GA

Preface - Embracing the Unexpected

The motivation behind penning the pages of "The Unexpected Stranger" stems from a deep-seated desire to open up my life, thoughts, and experiences. This is not crafted to cause harm; rather, it is a heartfelt endeavor to share my story — shaped by past journeys and guided by present and future aspirations.

This book is a testament to the power of stories to connect us on a profound level. It is a beacon for those who seek solace in others' trials and triumphs, reassuring them they are not alone in their difficulties. Through my words, I aim to break the silence that often shrouds personal battles, fostering a sense of community among those who have quietly endured their emotional struggles.

I aspire to offer a source of inspiration and support to those facing similar challenges; this is not merely a recounting of events, but a call to embrace one's narrative and find strength in sharing their truths.

"The Unexpected Stranger" is an invitation to explore the nuances of human experience, confront life's unexpected twists, and recognize the resilience within us all. I hope that, through the pages of this book, a dialogue will be sparked, and a sense of understanding will be cultivated among those who have kept silent about their struggles.

Realizing that someone you considered close is not the person they seemed to be, can be an intensely disorienting and emotionally tumultuous journey. The initial stages are often characterized by disbelief, as the facade of the person you thought you knew begins to crumble.

Whether it's a partner, a spouse, a family member, a co-worker, or a close friend, the revelation sends shockwaves through the foundation of trust that has been meticulously built over time. Questions of authenticity and the veracity of shared experiences start to unravel, leaving a trail of confusion and heartache.

The process feels like navigating a maze of emotions, as you wrestle with the stark contrast between the image they projected and the reality that unfolds.

As you come to terms with the unsettling truth, there's a profound sense of loss, not only for the relationship itself but also for the version of the person you believed existed. The journey to healing requires a delicate balance of self-reflection, forgiveness, and the difficult task of rebuilding trust, all while struggling with the profound shift in your perception of those closest to you. This complexity deepens when one is unaware of one's own emotions and struggles. In the end, the experience becomes a poignant reminder of the complexities inherent in human connections and the unpredictable nature of the paths we walk alongside others.

Encountering an unexpected stranger in a relationship refers to the revelation that the person you thought you knew well—whether a friend, partner, or acquaintance—turns out to be significantly different from the image they portrayed or the expectations you had. This realization often involves discovering unfamiliar aspects of their personality, values, or life circumstances that were previously undisclosed or not apparent. The term underscores the surprising and sometimes unsettling nature of discovering hidden or previously unknown facets of someone you are closely connected to.

To put it in another way, encountering an unexpected stranger in a relationship is like discovering a puzzle piece that doesn't fit the picture you thought you knew. It goes beyond mere quirks; implying a fundamental misalignment between who you believed your partner to be and who they truly are.

This often unfolds gradually, as subtle inconsistencies and hidden aspects of a person's identity surface. It might manifest as unanticipated behavior, undisclosed life choices, or a misalignment of values that were previously hidden. The experience can be disorienting, as the familiar terrain of a relationship transforms into uncharted territory.

This revelation doesn't necessarily imply bitterness or hostility on the part of the individual. Instead, it reflects the complexity of human nature and the subtle qualities that make each person unique.

The unexpected stranger in a relationship challenges preconceived notions and prompts a reassessment of not only the person in question but also the dynamics and foundations of the relationship itself.

Navigating this revelation requires balancing introspection, communication, and sometimes, difficult decisions. It's an opportunity for personal growth, both individually and as partners, as the relationship transforms in the face of newfound understanding. Though encountering an unexpected stranger can be emotionally challenging, it can also open the door to a deeper and more authentic connection—**if both parties are willing to navigate the complexities with empathy and openness.**

Chapter 1 – Roots, Sparks and Disappointments

Born and raised in the bustling big city, I was a spirited, young, pretty girl who was bubbly, curious, imaginative, and playful along with a sense of love, care, protection, and security. My upbringing was under the love and nurturing guidance of caring and good-looking parents, and I shared the joys of childhood with three handsome brothers.

In the environment I grew up in, adults often refrained from sharing their experiences, fearing judgment and other concerns. At times, guidance on relationships was given, and understanding had to be drawn from observing the behavior of parents and other relatives, from information shared by others, or from reading books. Learning from the streets was also a part of the experience, helping us navigate the complexities of relationships and life.

Growing up in a private Christian academy from childhood through college, my insights into relationships developed through interactions with classmates, exposure to television and literature, and again books. Many of us were sheltered or just naive. Upon entering college, an experience resembling a sex education course further enriched your understanding.

My parents dedicated themselves to providing the best possible preparation for marriage based on their experiences.

In my first year of college, I opted not to explore dating even though men were pursuing me. My focus was on acclimating to the college environment, spending time with friends, and dedicating myself to auditioning for a renowned choir, which kept me occupied. However, in the second year, I found myself continuously pursued by a young man I wasn't particularly interested in. Despite remaining open to the possibility of other relationships, this persistent hunter eventually became my boyfriend through college.

As our relationship continued to flourish, I was prepared to make significant sacrifices for my charming and handsome partner. I relocated to a sizable southern state where we aimed to secure employment, establish our residences, and acquire vehicles. This move was intended to provide us with the chance to assess whether we were inclined to pursue marriage. After two years, I inquired about his aspirations and what he wanted to pursue. When I saw the hesitation, I said, "I see you are having second thoughts, no problem."

I told him I no longer needed to live there; I was going home. Within a few days, he was asking my Dad for my hand in marriage. I told him, he was not obligated to marry me I was not desperate to marry.

He expressed his readiness to marry me, but a family member later suggested otherwise. Seeking clarity, I confronted him for an honest response, leading to some tension. Despite his reassurances, I remained skeptical, contemplating leaving the big southern city. However, he convinced me that I was the one and how much he loved me, etc. Therefore, we proceeded with our marriage plans, culminating in a grand wedding celebration on my parents' anniversary.

As we stepped into marriage, the image he initially presented to me was meticulously crafted, concealing hidden secrets that gradually began to surface. Initially, he spent quality time with me, but then he took on this second job, resulting in less and less time together. Having a second job would allow us to accomplish our goals and dreams, I thought. By our second year of marriage, I discovered, without plunging into specifics, that this second job was actually freeing him to carry on with another woman. This pattern continued with more women, leading to a series of infidelities that brought forth sorrow, pain, and tears.

Confronting him and seeking guidance through prayers, I battled with the realization that I felt unloved, alone, and trapped in the bed I had made. My family and friends heard less from me, and friends who visited noted a noticeable shift in the person they once knew.

Feeling a profound sense of embarrassment and deep emotional wounds, I discovered that I was spending the majority of my time in solitary reflection.

Amidst this challenging period, some members of his family, who held a genuine affection for me, extended their support by paying me visits. Their presence served as a source of encouragement, offering solace during a time of personal difficulty. We also began picking up some unhealthy habits because they knew what my husband was doing.

Despite my endeavors to fulfill the role of a devoted loving wife, my husband, who had declared his love and recited wedding vows to me, essentially he became distant. Yes, he was hardly available. When he came home it was to check on me and see what was going on. And he would ask me for money to say he would pay it back. That never happened. So, the money that I was saving kept depleting. Mind you, he never disclosed how much he earned at his job and was firmly against having a joint account. If we had one, I would see how he was spending his money—and that was clearly off-limits!

I was an accountant, so I wanted better for us. Yes, we talked about this before marriage and we were supposed to be on the same page but after the I-dos, things changed. I began to realize he was a taker and not a giver. I was becoming emotionally drained, and I had nothing to show for it. We were going to church together and that stopped.

I thought about how, when I graduated from college, my dad gave me a car as my graduation gift and talked about buying us a home. The home didn't happen because of my husband. So, blessed with my car, of course, I wanted to share it with my husband until he purchased him a vehicle. As I was told, he used my car to see another woman.

One day, coming home from work I was in a bad car accident, pinning my knees and jerking my back and neck. I appreciate him and his brother helping me out. After I received a settlement for my vehicle that was demolished, for the first time I was able to purchase my new car from the showroom floor. By this time, he had purchased a car and then a van. With all the time taken from my job for physical therapy, I lost my job so there was no money coming in for me. I asked my husband to help me financially to keep my vehicle as I looked for another job. Excited to begin my new accounting role, I hurried to where I'd parked my car, and to my dismay, it had been repossessed.

I had to take the bus to work. In the 80s where I was living, the transit was terrible unlike what I was accustomed to in the big city where I grew up.

Did I mention my husband had two vehicles that he kept clean and looking good and he didn't offer me not one of them?

As I think back, there were so many things that happened in this marriage. What got to me the most was the verbal abuse. What is verbal abuse, you may ask?

Verbal abuse means using words to hurt, control, or put someone down. It's more than just arguments; it's a repeated way of talking that makes the person feel bad about themselves, messes with their feelings, and tries to make them do what the abuser wants.

Having indulged in numerous pity parties including unhealthy habits, engaging in solo activities, and attending church alone when I was able to get a ride, I sought God's guidance on the course of action. Battling a multitude of overwhelming emotions, I sought solace in extended travels. While this served as a temporary escape, it delayed confronting the underlying issues.

Despite the emotional turmoil, the experiences of travel allowed me to find moments of joy and connection with family and friends. However, upon returning from these trips, a painful revelation awaited me – I discovered that he had been entertaining other women in our shared home during my absences.

The emotional rollercoaster continued as he would manipulate the situation, uttering sweet words to reconcile when transitioning between these encounters, drawing me into a cycle of forgiveness.

It was during a prolonged stay in the creative capital of the world for a wedding, that I began to notice physical changes – persistent fatigue and unrelenting hunger – which, unbeknownst to me at the time, hinted at a deeper and more complex layer of the unfolding narrative.

At the time, I was 5'8" and weighed 165 lbs, so when the notion of pregnancy was casually mentioned, I immediately dismissed it. Surely, it couldn't be true.

But once I returned home from other travels, the thought lingered, growing into a haunting presence that I couldn't shake.

Driven by a growing sense of uncertainty, I decided to seek confirmation from a doctor.

After undergoing a blood test, the doctor delivered the surprising news – I was indeed pregnant. This revelation collided with my plans to shed another 10 lbs for my envisioned ideal weight. The reality hit harder as I learned that I was already four and a half months into the pregnancy. Overwhelmed with conflicting emotions, I retreated to my car and allowed my tears to flow. The complexity of the situation unfolded – I was carrying a child with a man who didn't seem to love or care for me.

7

However, amidst the emotional chaos, a moment of clarity struck me, I was on the brink of becoming a mother, a happy thought that filled me with excitement, joy, and happiness.

Having played a role in helping my mother raise my siblings, nurturing dolls as a child, and loving my nieces and nephews, this was a tangible and genuine opportunity to embrace motherhood. Yet, the daunting task remained – how would I break the news to a husband who I knew harbored no desire for children?

When my husband was at home, it was rarely for me; rather, he would seek refuge with me when the woman he was involved with discovered his marital status, and his lies and gave him the boot.

When he came back and saw my face, he knew the truth – I was pregnant. I told him firmly, 'I'm having this baby with or without you. I know this child will bring love and care into my life; this is my gift from God.' I urged him to see it as a chance to embrace fatherhood.

Despite my focus on our baby, my husband remained unchanged. A wise family member advised me to shift my attention toward my own happiness and well-being for the sake of our child, leaving my husband's transformation in God's hands.

During family visits, my husband would play the role of a committed partner at home, creating a façade that he lived with me.

This experience taught me a crucial lesson about toxic relationships – be wary of men who discourage you from sharing your struggles with others. They want you to endure their mistreatment silently and bear the weight of their actions alone. However, my expressions gave away my inner turmoil, revealing my unhappiness despite the facade I was expected to maintain.

Five years into our marriage, a precious gift from God graced my life—the birth of our baby boy. Despite the challenges, I chose to endure an additional two years in a faltering marriage, holding onto hope and fervently praying that my husband would embrace his role as both a spouse to me and a father to our son. My sincere desire was to see my marriage thrive, fueled by the love I still held for him.

My marriage didn't go as I thought it would. Looking back, I realized I was so in love with him, but he didn't reciprocate my feelings.

Regrettably, even after a significant period of five years in a dating relationship and seven years of marriage, the impact on my emotions brought about waves of heartbreak, mental suffering, and pain. My heart was breaking from feeling unloved by him and knowing he was involved with other women. The ultimate betrayal came when he was with someone I considered a friend. I was overwhelmed with unhappiness and emotional exhaustion, struggling to understand how he could do this to me.

Despite the investment of time and commitment on my part, the foundation of our relationship endured an expected fracture, leaving me struggling with the fragmented pieces of what was once a seemingly solid connection. I started receiving phone calls about where my husband was! Mercy!

I asked myself. Why subject me to the torment of this emotional chaos if genuine love is absent? Wouldn't it be more human to grant me the freedom to chart my course forward?

The lingering uncertainty leaves me feeling like a pawn, manipulated in the tangled web of feelings and circumstances. It turns out his sole reason for holding on to this precarious connection was our son. There was absolutely no need for him to choose this path. He could have continued to be part of his son's life without creating unnecessary complications. His relationship with our son was never in question. It's disheartening to acknowledge that some individuals choose to lead others on a tumultuous ride, a rollercoaster of emotions that can leave enduring scars.

Navigating the complexities of healing and self-discovery in the aftermath of such significant and unexpected confusion. There were people from the church who would pick my son and me up to attend church, after-church Bible studies and other days grocery shopping. Yes, he possessed two vehicles, leaving my son and me to rely on public transportation or seek rides from others. It was only when a family member pointed out to him in disgust, that he realized the significance of the situation.

How could he not ensure that his wife had access to a car for daily transportation? This emphasized the lack of consideration for our practical needs and the disparities in our access to resources. This oversight not only highlighted an imbalance but also underscored the importance of thoughtful consideration in a marital partnership.

It was through those weekly Bible studies and fellowship that I saw how God truly loved me and gave me the strength and knowledge to make some changes in my life. Jesus Christ forgave me of my sins.

Nevertheless, through earnest prayers and in-depth Bible studies, we spoke about covenants with God. So, I made a covenant with the Lord that only He and I knew about. When you pray to God in silence, the enemy cannot hear.

Within two weeks my prayers were answered. It was clear that it was time to bring my marriage to a close. I cried with tears of joy that God had freed me from this toxic relationship. I asked God for what I needed, and He made it happen. God blessed me with a car and with my son, the clothes and things we could take with us, plus $200, I was off to another southern city. It was a heartbreaking realization that he had become an unexpected stranger.

Continuing to be guided by God, as I mentioned, I moved to a prominent southern city and experienced significant personal growth over the subsequent 15 years. As I rediscovered myself, having felt lost, three potential partners approached me with the talk of marriage within the first five years. However, feeling unprepared for such commitments, I chose to remain single. I desired to embrace my solitude despite facing inquiries about my choice not to marry. Throughout this period, blessings flowed, presenting moments of joy, happiness, and challenges.

I succeeded in gathering and acknowledging my emotions—both positive and negative—initiating a journey toward self-love and healing while raising my son. With heartfelt gratitude, I thank God for the multitude of family and friends who supported us throughout this journey.

As my son grew, I had to juggle two jobs to keep my son in Christian education through the 8th grade. The private school noticed my exhaustion, seeing me pick up my son before heading to my second job. I would sit in the car sleeping waiting for him, then make sure he had dinner before rushing out the door again. One day, the school inquired about my situation, asking what funds were needed. They asked if blessing me with monthly support would allow me to stay home with my child in the evenings. I said yes, and thus, I was blessed with the funds to quit my second job. I praise God for that school and the two individuals who showed such kindness.

After moving from apartments to a townhome, the Lord blessed us with a new home right in time for my son to start his high school years. From his new Christian high school, I had a huge bill for 9th grade, which my son's father didn't help cover. I had to pick up and drop my son from school and provide lunch as well. I still had to get with parents in my area to take my son to high school and/or take him home. Some parents weren't going home so I had to leave my job to pick him up, this wasn't always good in the eyes of my boss. I asked for a raise and the answer came back, why don't you put him in public school?

I was raised in Christian education from first grade through college. I wanted my son to have the same experience. After much prayer, the best choice was to take him out of unaffordable Christian education and put him in a public high school. It would be my responsibility to teach him about God from home. So, the school bus would pick him up and bring him home. They also had a special lunch program where I didn't have to pay.

My career in accounting and business administration flourished, and I found myself achieving significant milestones, after two vehicles giving up the ghost lol, I was the proud owner of a new car, affectionately named Black Beauty. This success marked the fruits of my professional achievements and opened up exciting opportunities for travel and fun.

As my son approached high school graduation, I became open to the idea of a second marriage. Through prayer and studying the Bible for guidance, new possibilities emerged. However, I faced unexpected challenges in preparing for a life partner.

Despite making some serious mistakes during my 15 years as a single parent, a reconnection with my God guided me to rectify my life. I dedicated my heart, mind, body, and soul, as well as my home, to God, seeking forgiveness and a renewed beginning.

As I readied myself for the prospect of entering into a new marriage, my prayers took on a specific focus. I earnestly sought continuous happiness, contentment, and fulfillment in my role as a single and celibate woman, dedicated to nurturing my handsome son as he transformed into a young man. Concurrently, I found myself on a journey of self-discovery, learning the nuances of being a good wife and fostering a healthy, loving relationship.

Throughout this period, I made a conscious effort to wholeheartedly embrace the various aspects of my life. From the joys of motherhood to the pursuit of personal fulfillment, every facet of my existence became an opportunity for growth and celebration.

Amidst my aspirations for a new marital chapter, I placed unwavering trust in God's guidance. Recognizing the significance of divine intervention, I would hope for the right life partner with a sense of patience and confidence that the future holds a promising and fulfilling union.

A couple of years before my son graduated from high school, I was pursued by a persistent handsome older man I vaguely remembered from our shared church attendance years ago.

He seemed genuinely nice, quiet, and godly, and we discovered a common history of attending the same church, even though we hadn't truly known each other. I knew him from a roommate who used to date him years before.

I pictured a life companion who cherished the Lord and would extend that love to both me and my son, a man who truly understood me. I envisioned a partner with a business sense to operate a venture benefiting others, someone financially savvy and passionate about creating ministries. Together, we would explore the world, sharing a common goal of helping others. I've waited patiently for 15 years for a man who embodies these qualities! Despite my reservations, (oh boy) I gave the determined suitor a chance, maintaining a certain distance for about two years. Mind you, no one else is pursuing me.

I immersed myself in another book called, "Act Like a Lady, Think Like a Man," by Steve Harvey. It talks about relationship insights, men's perceptions, self-empowerment, humor, and personal experiences.

I prayed, sensing that God was guiding me toward this man. My approach differed significantly from my first marriage.

Despite my initial belief that he was a nice, well-dressed, prayerful, godly man with experience in raising four children—seemingly possessing maturity, a strong work ethic, and potential for personal growth. It wasn't until later that I discovered he was very different from the man he portrayed himself to be.

Over the years, it became increasingly clear that he, too, struggled with uncertainty about his authentic self. Do you discern a recurring pattern? Consequently, another unforeseen stranger makes their way into my life!

Chapter 2 - The Normalcy of Daily Life

The normalcy of daily life is all about the regular schedules we follow every day, like waking up, going to work or school, spending time with family and friends, and relaxing in the evenings. It's the familiar routine that gives us a sense of existence, providing comfort and making us feel at ease in our surroundings.

In a relationship's daily rhythm, there's something special about waking up to the same face every day, sharing meals, and doing things together that bring you closer. These shared moments build a collection of memories that make your bond stronger over time.

Stability in a relationship isn't only about sharing a routine with a person—it's about feeling emotionally secure. It's knowing that no matter what happens, you can count on each other for support.

Our acquaintance spans approximately two years from a chance encounter at a single ministry event within our church community. As one of the leaders in it, I actively participated in events that brought together members from various churches. These gatherings were consistently anticipated, not with the only aim of finding a life partner, but as opportunities to expand our circle of friends. Our focus was on creating a diverse atmosphere, reaching out to individuals who might otherwise spend their time alone.

Reflecting on those times, the events were nothing short of epic. One memorable instance occurred at a book signing, where I unexpectedly encountered someone I hadn't seen in years. He had one of his friends with him. He introduced himself. I reciprocated the greeting, expressing that it was genuinely nice to make his acquaintance.

Eventually, I went about my business since I was actively involved in organizing the event. However, he continued to attend other gatherings hosted by the single ministry.

It became evident to me that he was a handsome, older, charming well-dressed man with a noticeable shyness and beautiful smile. Given my outgoing nature, I extended an invitation to him to join my table, just as I did with others entering the door. I can't recall exactly how he got my number, but he started calling me nonetheless.

Isn't it strange how life surprises us sometimes? We wound up working together on a business project. Someone we both knew hinted that this guy might like me. At first, I shrugged it off, saying I didn't have time for dating. But he didn't give up. He kept calling now and then for about two years, even though I wasn't sure about him.

So, how does this tie into the routine and stability of our relationship? Well, it all began when we first crossed paths. As we eventually ventured into the realm of dating, we opted to keep it low-key. Drawing inspiration from a popular book I was reading at the time, which advocated getting to know each other over the phone.

The approach of connecting on the phone allowed for open and honest conversations, creating a space where we could freely express what was on our minds. Following the book's suggestion, I took the initiative to ask questions and encouraged him to share his thoughts, diligently noting down his responses.

Our dates typically took place on weekends, and by keeping our conversations rather simple, we maintained a casual and easygoing dynamic. The financial aspect of our outings was shared, with him often taking the lead but occasional contributions from my end. Prayer became a significant part of our connection, a ritual we embraced during our phone conversations. In those moments we discovered the depth of our communication, realizing that we could discuss anything and everything with ease.

We began discussing our childhoods, past relationships, marriages, children, aspirations, dreams, and ministry involvement to get to know each other better. In the spirit of transparency, we openly addressed topics such as health, medications, debt, and credit scores.

With numerous prayers, unwavering faith, and trust in God, we reached a point where we felt ready to make our relationship public. I went to the extent of bringing him to family events, allowing my relatives to assess him before I allowed my emotions to become entangled.

One thing I really enjoyed was having friends over after church, so I started inviting him to those gatherings. It was important for me to see how he interacted with other people and how he fit into my social circle. Seeing him in different situations helped me get a better sense of who he was beyond just our one-on-one time. It was like putting all the pieces of the puzzle together to see the bigger picture of our relationship.

It was a surprising yet beautiful moment of my life—a year into our relationship, we were taking a leisurely stroll at our church picnic when suddenly, he got down on one knee. He said the sweetest things and then asked me the most important question: "Will you marry me?" I didn't even need to think twice; my heart was overflowing with joy, and without hesitation, I replied with a resounding "Yes." It was a moment filled with love, happiness, and the promise of a beautiful future together.

But little did I know that the fairy tale I had imagined with the man I would soon marry wouldn't be the one I expected. It's funny how our expectations can sometimes be so different from reality.

Being in a relationship brings about the good, the bad, and the ugly—the pros and cons. I always felt like our bond was something special. Even though there was a nine-year age gap between us, it never seemed to matter. We both just clicked, and if anything, we seemed to defy the usual signs of aging.

After much thought and prayer, I revisited my checklist again, weighing the practical reasons for marrying him and making sure everything aligned. But then it dawned on me—marriage isn't about checking off every box on a list. In fact, can we ever truly check all of them off? What matters most often goes beyond the list. It wasn't just about the feelings in my heart; I was thinking more with my head. I wanted a man who would love me more than I loved him, a contrast to my first marriage, where I was so in love, but he wasn't with me. I loved him too much, and I couldn't repeat that in a second marriage, I thought. We talked about what each of us could bring to the marriage and envisioned ourselves as a power couple, built on mutual love, and respect and guided by faith.

Our engagement was short. We thought, hey, we're not exactly spring chickens anymore, so why wait around for two years? Plus, we'd been getting to know each other long before we made it official. We were engaged by the summer.

Before saying "I do," we made a pact to go through six weeks of marriage counseling. During that time, we addressed any issues that popped up and came up with strategies for handling them. Honesty was key for us—we made sure to keep it real with each other every step of the way.

During our engagement and marriage counseling, I saw firsthand how determined he was. He worked tirelessly to gather the funds we needed for our wedding, and together, we made sure everything was covered. I admired his faith in God, his potential, and his strong work ethic. Talking to him seemed to be easy—we had genuine conversations, and our affection for each other just flowed naturally. He had this charming shyness about him, and, well, he wasn't too hard on the eyes either. We even entertained the idea of starting a business together. Sure, he had a habit of running a little late sometimes, like many others do, but we always made time for heartfelt discussions about our future aspirations and dreams.

We celebrated our union in the autumn season surrounded by our loved ones, both family and friends. Our honeymoon was for a week in the entertainment capital of the world.

Before getting married, it was just my son and me. Our living situation shifted when a family of four moved in. It was supposed to be a temporary situation, but it turned out to have lasted longer than I expected. Contrary to my initial request for them to relocate as soon as possible. With my new husband moving in, it shifted the household dynamic drastically. This situation posed a hindrance for any newly married couple, especially when privacy was scarce. This wasn't what I had in mind. When I think about starting a life together as a couple, I imagine doing it side by side, facing whatever comes our way together.

During the time my son lived with us, he maintained a steady job. After my vehicle was wrecked, we were fortunate to borrow the family of four's car, which allowed me to drop him off at the park and ride and pick him up afterward. I admired his sense of responsibility as he contributed to household expenses by offering to pay rent and his willingness to help with chores around the house.

Despite our best efforts to overcome the daily challenges of others living with us, things were tough. Emotions were running high, and it felt like we were up against impossible odds. I just wanted it to be my husband and son in our home. These were the two most important men in my life, and my Daddy too!

It was really hard on my son—he felt like he was on an emotional roller coaster, and the tension between all of us was really wearing him down.

He could see how everyone wanted me, his mom to take their side, putting me in an impossible situation. He noticed how hard I was trying to make things work with everyone, but it was just stressing me out even more.

But eventually, things reached a breaking point, and my son decided to leave earlier than I had hoped, which just made everything even more complicated. It had been just my son and me for most of his life, and we had a really strong bond. He's been living in that house since he was 10 years old.

Sadly, my husband didn't seem to value the bond between my son and me, and his actions showed it. While I won't get into all the specifics, there are many instances that my husband seems to have forgotten, but I have photos to remind me. He kept saying he treated my son like his own, but the actions didn't match up. There were hardly any texts or calls to my son unless he had something critical to say. I knew because he treated me the same way. It made me wonder if he never experienced love growing up, which is why he couldn't give it to us. We were a package deal—I wanted my son to know what it's like to have a caring stepdad, especially since he didn't have one growing up. It was deeply disappointing and hurtful to see the lack of love and support for my son, who was such an important part of my life. My son's choice to leave caught me by surprise, but I could see why he felt it was necessary.

Originally, the plan was for him to stay at the house as long as he worked, contributed to expenses, and pursued his education. This was discussed during our engagement. We thought this would give him the chance to save up for a car and his place. In my upbringing, we always supported our children to help them succeed. However, my spouse had a different upbringing where once you started working, you were expected to fend for yourself outside the family home. That is what makes you a man. It seemed like my husband said one thing but did another through his actions. It was like he flipped a switch on our agreement before and after marriage. My son's sudden decision to leave what we had agreed upon left me feeling incredibly saddened, discouraged, and isolated.

Now that my son has moved on, I'm feeling more and more unloved, trapped between two men battling for control of the household—one my husband, the other the head of the family of four. And yet, it's my name on the mortgage! It's as if their struggle for dominance overshadows my place in the home, leaving me stuck in the crossfire of a fight that shouldn't even exist.

With my son moving out and my husband struggling to find steady work, along with the family of four not really contributing financially, our family's financial situation became difficult. We were relying on my son's income and my unemployment benefits to make ends meet. Without a consistent source of income from my husband, things were challenging for us financially.

One of my friends, also married to an older man, suggested that my husband file for Social Security. This turned out to be a blessing from God. We began receiving a monthly stipend that included retirement benefits.

Finding myself in a difficult situation, I pondered the unfortunate circumstances before we married surrounding a car accident that left my vehicle which I called "Black Beauty" completely damaged, rendering me without any means of transportation. Compounding the issue was our geographical distance from individuals we knew could extend a helping hand, amplifying the sense of isolation. Thank God my spouse had a vehicle!

Facing this setback, I decided to explore alternative income roots to manage our financial issues. Recognizing the potential of remote work, I searched for opportunities that allowed me to contribute to our household income from the comfort of our home. My spouse finally secured a stable job, bringing much-needed relief and a sense of stability to our lives.

As my savings dwindled, I reached a point where I could no longer cover the mortgage payments. Despite my efforts to refinance the home, I encountered an unforeseen challenge—no company seemed willing to take on the task, leaving me perplexed and frustrated. Turning to my faith, I sought guidance, and through what can only be described as a divine intervention, my home being in a revocable trust proved to be a blessing. This fortunate circumstance allowed us to continue residing in the home for an additional three years with no mortgage payments. This was nothing but the grace of God!

While this was a big help, it would have been even better if the head of the family of four understood our financial struggles and chipped in with rent, but he didn't. This added more stress to an already tough financial situation.

My husband and I were overwhelmed with confusion and uncertainty, not sure what to do about the situation with the other family. We prayed for guidance and reached out to a pastor we trusted, who knew both families well. He gave us some helpful advice, telling us to be honest and stick to the facts when talking things out. Following this counsel, we spoke up about our concerns with the leader of the stayed family, which didn't go over well and strained our relationship. Eventually, they finally decided to move.

Once it was just my spouse and I, we felt a sense of relief. The house was calm, and we could talk to each other without distractions. But my husband kept bringing up the difficulties we encountered, initiating a cycle of blame and negativity without taking any ownership.

Having moments to review the first years of our marriage was challenging. I found myself bearing witness to the gradual transformation of a man I didn't recognize. I keenly observed his interactions with the others in the house on how he gained insights into, how he navigated various situations and there were many. This revealed facets of his character that were previously unknown to me.

I sought advice, and I was told to talk it out with my husband and then give it six months, after which we shouldn't bring it up again. I thought about it: five years of dealing with issues with others in the house versus just talking about it for six months. I didn't need six months if I was ready to move on after just one month. But it seemed like my husband wanted to keep rehashing everything at every opportunity, and it was exhausting.

I saw no reason to prolong the situation for months without resolution; I simply wanted to move forward. I began to wonder, "Where is the love?" The frequency of our arguments and disagreements grew, creating emotional distance between us. His behavior changed—he started coming home late, appeared more fatigued, stayed up late watching television, and devoted significant time to his ministry. As a result, our time together became increasingly scarce.

In an effort to seek guidance again, we engaged in marriage counseling with a Christian couple, initially showing promise but eventually reverting to familiar patterns. We reviewed everything that was on his mind including the first five years of marriage, he was in a cycle that never ended no matter how many apologies and asking forgiveness was given. It became more negative than positive. I was tired of fighting for something that my spouse could not get over.

Moving forward means wiping the slate clean, like putting a fresh coat of paint on a wall. It's a chance to begin anew, and there's something really exhilarating about that. You get to leave the past behind and look ahead to what's next with anticipation and optimism.

As we adjusted to living together as a couple, he frequently insisted on having things go his way, and when they didn't, his reactions were often extreme and unreasonable. This exposure raised personal concerns and unease within me. There were instances where his anger seemed to transform into something unsettling, almost as if a different, darker side of him emerged. I became frightened. His incessant yelling, screaming, and whining became overwhelming. Let me say this, if you were to encounter him, you might question if you're referring to the same person.

He had a remarkable ability to present a calm and composed image to the outside world, hiding the complexities and struggles that occurred in private. Once again, I found myself questioning, "Where is the love I'm supposed to feel?" Women instinctively know when they're truly loved and cherished, and when they do, they naturally return that love to their partners. It's about feeling valued and appreciated— something everyone deserves in a relationship.

Frustration overwhelmed me as I yearned for a listening ear and empathetic support. While I acknowledge that my communication may not have been ideal, possibly coming across as harsh in expressing my emotions, the underlying emotions of anger mixed with unhappiness fueled my attempts to seek understanding from others.

Regrettably, placing my trust in individuals whom I thought would provide a reliable support system turned out to be useless. The expected assistance I longed for remained out of reach, intensifying the sense of entrapment that enveloped me anew.

In moments of vulnerability, the need for a listening ear and genuine assistance becomes crucial. I yearned for a connection with people who could offer the emotional and practical support I sought. It wasn't about mere sympathy but a genuine desire for someone to comprehend my struggles and extend a helping hand. Unfortunately, the reality fell short of these expectations.

In times, when sharing one's burdens becomes essential, the question arises: beyond seeking encouragement in faith, who can one turn to? It would be immensely valuable to find individuals who possess the capacity to empathize, understand, and provide tangible assistance.

The search for companionship becomes a quest for genuine connections that go beyond words, reaching into the realm of compassionate actions. It highlights the importance of building meaningful relationships with people who will stand by you in times of need, offering real strength and encouragement, not just superficial gestures.

God truly knows what you need! Thankfully, a couple of my old girlfriends, who've known me for a long time, reached out to me. They listened to me, shared their thoughts, offered support, and even prayed with me. Their love and support meant the world to me. I'm so grateful for their genuine care, friendship, and sisterhood.

Faced with the storms of mental distress, I turned to emotional eating, resulting in a 30-pound weight gain. The physical strain manifested through tension headaches that eventually turned into migraines, a clear sign of the toll on my well-being. I realized then that my deep longing for a true relationship was not only destroying my mental health but also taking a serious toll on my body. Trust, a crucial element, had been shattered, consistency was sorely lacking, and the emotional connection between us had significantly weakened. The plea for divine intervention became a turning point in my quest for clarity and resolution.

Family concerns arose during a gathering when one of my husband's sons expressed worries about his father possibly experiencing PTSD. This got me thinking, so I did some digging. PTSD, a mental health condition rooted in traumatic experiences, can manifest in many ways—emotionally, mentally, and physically. People may feel anxious, and fearful, or experience flashbacks of the event, while their thoughts might become negative or distorted. It can disrupt sleep and lead them to avoid reminders of the trauma, affecting daily life and relationships. PTSD impacts people differently and to varying degrees, highlighting its complexity and profound effect on mental health. Truly understanding PTSD means examining both its immediate impact and its long-term effects.

Mercy, mercy, mercy! My eyes were suddenly opened to the reality of the man I had married – he had been struggling with mental illness all these years. Determined to understand the implications, I looked into investigating what this revelation meant. It became evident that my husband's upbringing, past marriage, raising his children as a single working parent, and diverse professional experiences had significantly influenced the complexities within his family.

Each of them played a role in this intricate story, carrying a piece of the puzzle that made up their collective history, marked by the complexities and nuances of their father's journey through life.

As I imparted this newfound understanding to two of his children, it brought into focus the complicated layers of their father's influence on their lives. It unveiled how he had shaped their upbringing, drawing from the lessons learned through the challenges of his first marriage, navigating other relationships, and the diverse array of his professional experiences. Their lives were intricately woven into the fabric of his own, forming part of the broader narrative of a family marked by complexities and imperfections. This revelation provided insight into the dynamics that contributed to what could be characterized as a dysfunctional family, each member bearing the imprints of their shared history and the unique journey of their father.

The most troubling revelation was that my husband remained oblivious to his own condition. Unbeknownst to him, he had been struggling with PTSD since the unnecessary Vietnam War in the 70s. In an effort to understand his medical history, I requested records from a hospital he frequented. These records revealed a history of frequent hospital visits predating our marriage. Unfortunately, the crucial step of seeking assistance from the VA hospital eluded him simply because he was unaware it was an option.

Noticing his frequent injuries at home or on the job, I questioned him once, asking, "Why aren't you seeking help from the VA hospital?" I was amazed that the hospital he had visited didn't send him to the VA hospital. It wasn't until another severe job-related accident occurred that I insisted him not to return home until visited the VA hospital. During this visit, they informed him that had he delayed seeking help, the situation might have led to the amputation of his leg.

Gratefully, he spent a few days in the hospital, and, thanks to divine intervention, he reached the hospital in time for crucial medical attention. I was there to support him, and they allowed me to spend the nights with him.

Following his discharge, fellow patients advised us to explore the possibility of VA Disability Benefits, a resource of which we were previously unaware. Engaging in extensive research, I discovered this option four years into our marriage, and my efforts to advocate for him played a pivotal role in him receiving these benefits. Glory to God! In a detailed letter to the VA claims, I encapsulated everything I knew about him from childhood to our marriage, which proved instrumental in the approval process. We express gratitude for this monthly income, which has proven to be invaluable.

In addition to struggling with untreated PTSD from the war, my husband endured other dramatic life events along the way plus the first five years of our marriage.

Let's look into the issue regarding the VA. My husband, a Vietnam veteran who fought on the front lines, brings to light the unfortunate reality that these courageous soldiers, who fought for our country, often did not receive the adequate treatment they deserved. They were insufficiently informed about accessing medical care at the VA Hospital or claiming the entitled monthly benefits.

As I crafted the letter for the VA, a myriad of revelations unfolded before me. My heart went out to all Vietnam veterans who remained unaware. When my husband returned from the war, he was irrevocably changed. A significant number of his friends experienced being shot or losing their lives during the war.

Struggling with childhood adversities, diminished self-esteem and confidence, loss of his photographic memory, and enduring mental strain, he emerged as a fractured man. Dysfunction became the norm for him and his family, yet they remained oblivious to it.

Consequently, he operated below his optimal capacity. Unaware of the illness he was wrestling with, he proceeded to marry and raise children.

Sensing that something was amiss but lacking guidance, he persisted through prayer, faith, and his best efforts in marriage and parenting. Unfortunately, his untreated mental illness persisted, leading to a divorce and his subsequent role as a single parent who worked long hours.

We all bear the burden of an imperfect childhood, defined by the unavoidable errors committed by our parents or, in certain cases, the absence of parental figures, resulting in an upbringing within foster homes or agencies. The diversity of our backgrounds becomes particularly evident when I reflect on my upbringing, which starkly contrasts with the experiences of the man I am now dealing with. He seems unaware of the brokenness within him, and this realization leaves me emotionally shattered.

The depth of my exasperation intensifies as I am confronted with the question of how to support him while feeling mentally drained. The challenge lies not only in his lack of awareness regarding his own struggles but also in the recognition that he may be incapable of reciprocating love in the manner I long for.

It's a painful realization that adds another layer of complexity to our relationship, prompting me to navigate the delicate balance between seeking his well-being and preserving my own mental and emotional health.

Chapter 3 - Investigating the Unexplained

Following the revelation that my spouse is struggling with post-traumatic stress disorder, I embarked on a journey of understanding, familiarizing myself with the symptoms, and observing various behaviors associated with this condition.

In my quest to navigate the details of this singular situation, I have devoted considerable time and effort to methodically record and document my endeavors.

The more I learned about this situation, the more overwhelmed I felt. I had hoped we could support each other, but it turns out we're both struggling with something similar. We haven't really experienced genuine love ourselves, so it's hard to give what we haven't received. Basically, he can't fully invest in our relationship because of his past issues, and I can only give so much because of his struggles. At some point, I realized we were both caught in a cycle of unhealed wounds, which made it impossible to build the deep connection I so desperately wanted.

I've been putting in the work to figure out why things feel so off between me and my spouse. I'm diving deep into every little detail of our connection and relation to each other. Asking for God's help, he's revealing most of the confusing bits and pieces so I can get a better grasp on what's really going on between us. It's all about gaining a clearer understanding of this unique situation I've found myself in.

I then began to take an active role in managing his healthcare, accompanying him to VA appointments, and ensuring he had the prescribed medications. While I encouraged his independence in various aspects, it became evident that he required assistance. I assumed the responsibilities of handling VA paperwork, scheduling appointments, and essentially became his secretary, also overseeing the smooth operation of our household which includes the finances.

His tendency to procrastinate and the prolonged decision-making process became apparent, prompting me to take charge of tasks that required immediate attention.

Despite our efforts to engage in counseling and apply the valuable insights we gained, navigating these lessons as a couple proved to be a challenging endeavor.

It became increasingly clear that, despite his genuinely kind heart, adventurous spirit, and thoughtful approach, there were certain areas where he struggled to meet my needs. During our conversations, a noticeable pattern emerged—he repeatedly returned to past events. While I longed to grow and move forward, he seemed stuck, anchored in old stories and unable to let go of the past.

He's all about wanting respect and making sure he's seen as the man in our relationship. But here's the thing – he can't keep his word, if you can't keep your word, how can there be trust? He seems to have a hard time admitting when he's wrong sometimes or when he's not able to do something. It's like there's a clash between his desire to be respected and his trouble seeing his limits like giving respect. This complex situation of how we deal with each other makes it tough to get on the same page about what we expect and what's really happening.

Communicating with him became increasingly difficult as he continually picked apart my actions, always insisting that his way was superior. I began to feel suffocated, with every aspect of my life being scrutinized. I genuinely wanted to stand by him and be supportive, but this constant pressure led me to seek comfort and guidance from a higher source—God.

He was fighting a real battle with his mental health. On one hand, he wanted to be the loving, supportive partner I needed, but on the other hand, he felt overwhelmed with frustration, anger, and sadness because he believed he was falling short. His pride made it even harder—he didn't want to admit he was struggling mentally, which left him feeling like he had to hide it. This only deepened his emotional struggles, creating a distance between us and making it more challenging to connect.

He expressed a desire to be involved in my life, seeking to understand my daily routines. However, due to the challenges posed by our conflicting schedules, this involvement became difficult. Despite our efforts to engage in discussions about major decisions, there are instances when he is unable to recall these conversations. This situation can be both challenging and frustrating, as it complicates our ability to move forward. When we can't align on our decisions, it often leads to misunderstandings and delays, preventing us from making progress together.

Navigating his struggles with work attendance and his sleep disorder presented additional complexities. I found myself encouraging him to prioritize rest when fatigued, suggesting stops at well-lit gas stations for brief naps lasting between 1 to 2.5 hours. As a result, his return home varied between 8 pm to 11 pm nightly, well after the household had settled for the night. In this exhausted state, he followed a routine of calming down with TV, addressing hunger, and preparing for bed ending in prayer. In observation, both his morning and evening rituals became a focal point, showcasing elements that could be considered beneficial and others that required significant improvement.

My unwavering belief in God and the power of prayer forms the cornerstone of my faith, providing a profound source of strength and peace. Despite the challenges that have come our way, I hold onto this trust and faith in God, acknowledging the blessings that have been bestowed upon us.

In the face of adversity, we strive to do everything within our means, embracing the idea that faith without action is incomplete. While challenges persist, trust and faith in God serve as guiding lights, inspiring us to persevere through difficulties with resilience and hope.

Our communication faces challenges, particularly in coordinating events or ensuring punctuality for work. His difficulty in adhering to schedules often led to us taking separate cars. Work posed another set of challenges, with his struggles to sleep at night and recurring nightmares, seemingly a lingering effect from his time in the war. Initially, this was deeply unsettling for me, but through careful study of his condition and discussions with his doctor, I learned effective coping mechanisms to deal with these aspects of his experience.

Upon realizing that my parents still resided in the bustling city but were slowing down and dealing with health issues, I decided to return home to check on them. Although a nurse regularly attended to their needs, I felt a more hands-on approach was necessary. I understood that Silent Generation parents often shy away from burdening their children with concerns over the phone. This made me recognize the need to be physically present to truly understand their situation. As the oldest and only daughter, I embraced the responsibility of caring for them and turned to prayer for the strength to manage this while running my household in my Southern city.

What started as brief visits evolved into prolonged stays, spanning weeks and even months, as my parents faced ongoing health challenges. During these extended periods, I dedicated myself to ensuring their affairs were in order, securing the best healthcare available, and doctor visits, helping them run errands, and arranging for a reliable and compassionate caregiver. This commitment persisted over several years.

However, while fulfilling my responsibilities, it became apparent that challenges emerged on the home front in the southern city.

Upon returning home, I found remnants of the carefully prepared meals I had left behind still in the refrigerator, along with costly untouched food service deliveries. It quickly became clear that household duties were not being managed effectively. I noticed weight gain and that he was not looking well, along with signs of neglect in the kitchen, which indicated that my absence was impacting the upkeep of our home.

He would often leave pots on the stove, forgetting about them until they reached varying degrees of heat, from low to medium to almost dangerously high, resulting in burnt pots. Filled with embarrassment, he would hide these incidents from me.

For example, he considered it acceptable to place a spoon in the microwave while heating his tea in a mug, resulting in sparks and leaving an imprint of the spoon inside the microwave. He said he did this all the time, and it was no big deal.

Sending him to the store or tasking him with picking up food became time-consuming endeavors, often taking hours for him to return. He lost his sense of urgency and frequently delayed simpler tasks. Over the years, this situation has shown some improvement. While such delays were not as pronounced in the earlier years of our marriage, they have become more prominent over time.

In my quest to comprehend more about my spouse, I accompanied him to the VA, where they recognized and acknowledged me as a caregiver for him. They introduced a monthly service for caregivers, proving to be beneficial.

Despite having a lot on my plate, juggling caregiving responsibilities not only for my husband but also for my veteran father and mother, I eventually started attending these meetings, albeit a couple of years later.

Within the realm of healthcare, the treatment one receives can sometimes be influenced by the perception of available support. Recognizing this, I took it upon myself to advocate for both my husband and my parents, firmly believing in the importance of standing in as a dedicated support for their well-being. Going to great lengths, I ensured that they not only received adequate care but strived for the best possible care available.

My commitment to this role was met with much respect within the healthcare community, a sentiment for which I am profoundly grateful. In every step of the journey, I attribute my ability to fulfill this duty to a higher power, expressing gratitude to God for the determination that empowered me to carry out this important responsibility.

The time and effort invested in understanding the person I am married to have been extensive. Balancing the complexities of caregiving for my husband, father, and mother has demanded a great deal of my attention, time, and energy. Yet, through these challenges, I've sought to foster a deeper understanding of my spouse and navigate the complexity of our relationship with empathy and resilience.

The diminishing quality of our time together as a couple underscored a widening gap in our understanding of the roles and expectations within our relationship. The envisioned role I had for him as the man of the home significantly deviated from his interpretation, intensifying the rift that was growing between us. This divergence in expectations contributed to a palpable sense of disconnection and discord in our lives.

Our lives, encompassing the realms of mental, physical, financial, and spiritual well-being, became intricately entwined with these evolving dynamics. The challenges we faced were not merely confined to the external aspects of life but permeated into the very core of our individual and shared experiences. Navigating this multifaceted terrain demanded a reassessment of our priorities, a realignment of expectations, and a concerted effort to bridge the widening gaps that threatened the foundation of our relationship.

Armed with this newfound knowledge, I have sought to navigate our relationship with empathy and sensitivity, recognizing the unique challenges that arise when supporting a loved one dealing with PTSD. My commitment to comprehending the peculiarities of this mental health condition has led me to engage in open communication, educate myself on effective coping mechanisms, and foster an environment of support and understanding within our shared life.

Chapter 4 - Confrontation and Denial

When you find yourself in the company of those who know you were growing up or as an adult, they often possess a unique perspective that reveals facets of your personality and behavior that may elude your own awareness. These close connections, who've been with you through thick and thin, really get you. They know your quirks and understand when things get tricky for you. It's like they can read your moves and know exactly how you roll in life.

In moments of shared presence, there can be a reflexive resistance to their observations. The inclination to deny or reject their insights arises, accompanied by thoughts like "That can't be me" or "I don't recognize myself in that way." This resistance stems from the discomfort of confronting aspects of ourselves that may not align with the idealized self-image we project to the world.

Sometimes facing up to these observations is tough, like swallowing a bitter pill. It goes against our wish to always show our best side to others. Finding out about behaviors or traits we didn't even realize we had can be unsettling. But hey, this journey of discovering more about us, even if it's sparked by what others notice, is important for your growth.

Recognizing that others may perceive us differently, and occasionally more objectively, opens the door to self-reflection and transformation. Embracing these insights, even when they contradict our self-perception, can lead to a deeper understanding of who we are and how we relate to the world.

It's a chance to get better, to be truer to ourselves, and to match up who we think we are with who we really are. Ultimately, the real test isn't in brushing off these eye-openers, but in bravely embracing them as sparks that ignite our personal growth.

My spouse's reluctance to recognize the urgency for treatment stemmed from his comfort with the person he had become over the years. He had grown accustomed to a certain way of life and hadn't fully connected the dots between his well-being and the potential for personal growth. While being a single parent his focus was working and raising his children thus remaining in his comfort zone. Being married to me brought about a different set of challenges as he struggled to comprehend what steps to take.

During our conversations, he perceived that I was singling him out as if I considered myself superior. However, I am well aware of my imperfections, having experienced various relationships, studied, and attended seminars. My intention was not to convey a sense of superiority but rather to express that something seemed out of place and to share my thoughts. I acknowledge that I needed to work on my delivery, but over the years, God has blessed me with significant improvements. Ultimately, years of persuasion and the insights of professionals led him to acknowledge his diagnosis, confirming what I had suspected all along.

The revelation was profound, shedding light on numerous aspects of his behavior and experiences. However, armed with this newfound knowledge, he found himself at a loss, uncertain about how to navigate the path of self-discovery that lay ahead.

For me, there was a sense of relief in finally understanding the underlying factors contributing to his challenges. The diagnosis provided a framework for comprehending the complexities we had been struggling with.

The journey ahead presented its own set of struggles, emphasizing the crucial role of treatment in addressing the identified issues. While the diagnosis brought clarity, the path to resolution required a commitment to therapeutic interventions, a process that would undoubtedly shape our shared future. The challenges, though significant, became opportunities for growth as we embarked on a course aimed at developing well-being and navigating the complexities inherent in his condition.

Over the years, attempts to initiate treatment were hindered by his demanding work schedule, making it nearly impossible for him to attend in-person sessions. Fast forward to the present, where virtual treatment options are available; however, the unpredictable nature of his occupation makes it difficult to commit to a set time for virtual appointments. Even with the best intentions, unforeseen work responsibilities can arise, causing him to miss scheduled sessions. As someone who thrives on being proactive, organized, analytical, a caregiver, and goal-oriented, I understand the importance of prioritizing mental health. Despite my efforts to encourage him to seek treatment, the constraints of his work and the unpredictability of his schedule have posed significant obstacles.

It's a delicate balance between advocating for his well-being and recognizing the demands of his professional life. The question that may be asked: Why is it challenging for him to take time off from work? Sifting through this matter reveals a fundamental difference in financial approaches within our relationship – the classic dynamic of a spender and a saver.

In this scenario, my partner epitomized the spender archetype once he was adept at depleting a two-week paycheck within a mere couple of days. There's a consistent pattern of spending where the same purchases occur, sometimes accompanied by additional acquisitions, leading to the accumulation of credit card debt. Despite harboring the belief that he can formulate strategies to replenish the funds, the actual outcome often diverges significantly from this optimistic perspective.

As a saver, I've noticed a recurring pattern: whenever funds are diligently set aside for unforeseen challenges, those challenges seem to manifest consistently. When my spouse refrains from spending following the budget, a shift in attitude occurs. There's an inclination for him to take control of the bills independently, aiming to allocate funds in a manner that aligns with personal spending preferences.

It becomes a delicate balance between individual spending preferences and the collective financial goals outlined in the budget. The desire for personal expenditure sometimes takes precedence, leading to fluctuations in adherence to the established financial plan. Striking a harmonious equilibrium between personal desires and financial discipline remains an ongoing challenge, necessitating consistent efforts to align individual spending habits with the overarching budgetary structure.

In navigating this financial terrain, the role of divine providence becomes evident. It is through the grace of God that we are sustained. While the spender-saver dynamic persists, it is the sustaining grace of God that empowers us to overcome challenges, pursue aspirations, and navigate the complexities of fiscal responsibility within the context of our shared dreams. On a more profound level, envision a scenario where both partners possess a clear understanding of the financial obligations involved in saving for home improvements, significant purchases, unexpected emergencies, or travel plans. They use a credit card to settle bills promptly, knowing funds are available in their account.

Despite economic challenges, saving is achievable if both are committed to prioritizing financial goals. It requires shared responsibility and a strategic approach to navigate today's economic landscape. Though it may seem daunting, disciplined financial planning can lead to a more secure and harmonious future.

I persist in undertaking prolonged stays to attend to the needs of my parents in another state, and it is consistently by God's blessings that we were provided with all that was needed. My parents and I are always grateful to my husband for his unwavering support and understanding during my extended stays, which often lasted weeks or even months, particularly during my parents' illnesses.

As we continue to answer the question: Why is it challenging for him to take time off from work? My spouse must have structure. If my husband is not employed, he often retreats to our bedroom or his man cave, claiming to be working. But unfortunately, the tasks around the house remain unaddressed. And these are the tasks we have agreed upon for weeks and months. I know he does tasks around the house that I don't know of, and I appreciate that.

During the week, I don't expect much, especially when he is working because he gets home so late. However, on Sundays, I hope we can

51

tackle some household chores or home improvements together. He often forgets how happy I am when we can work on projects as a team. However, he tends to delay starting these tasks until the late afternoon or early evening. For me, I want to complete my work earlier so that I can rest afterward or spend some quality family time.

As the rest of the household begins winding down for the evening, my spouse suddenly exhibits a burst of energy, attempting to accomplish what should have been done earlier in the day. This delayed burst of productivity involves the use of tools and rigorous movements, disrupting the tranquil atmosphere of the household.

The challenge lies in balancing responsibilities, especially when my extended stays demand a collective effort to manage household affairs. Despite my spouse's late working hours, I still expect him to perform household chores timely.

There are instances in our lives when the allure of pursuing different career paths becomes tempting, often driven by the belief that we can excel in areas beyond our current expertise. However, the reality may unfold in a way we never anticipated, revealing the importance of heeding the wisdom behind the adage, "stick with what you know." This realization often dawns upon us when it's too late, and the consequences of venturing into unfamiliar territories become apparent.

During periods marked by financial strain due to experimenting with new career avenues that failed to yield the expected results, the urgency to reassess and make pragmatic choices became evident. A mantra emerged: "If it doesn't work in 30 days, then seek alternative employment." Despite diligently applying this strategy for several months, the financial woes persisted, savings being used to assist in covering monthly expenses leading to a critical juncture where all I could do was cry out to God. Alternatively, he mentions contemplating leaving his job, seeking my opinion. We both concur that it's an inopportune moment, only for him to inform me later that he has indeed quit his job. The bombshell drops. My heart plummets. Naturally, this unfolded just as we were beginning to stabilize again!

In times of distress, turning to faith and seeking divine intervention can bring peace and direction. Recognizing the inherent wisdom and intuition bestowed upon women, there was a realization that relying on spiritual guidance could be a transformative step to navigate the challenges.

It is ingrained in a man, by the divine design of God, the inherent goodness of work. When a man is raised with the right values, he understands the profound responsibility of providing for his family. This ingrained understanding becomes a driving force, motivating him to work diligently and fulfill his role as a provider. It was acknowledged that, while men might desire unwavering support and deference, the strength of a woman's intuition and insight is a valuable asset. The challenge lay in balancing the need for autonomy with the desire to contribute meaningfully to the household.

There were moments of mutual recognition—a shared acknowledgment of the diverse roles and responsibilities we each shouldered to sustain our household. However, in the ups and downs of life, there were instances where the script seemed to get flipped, disrupting the seamless understanding we had established.

Navigating the complexities of communication, appreciation, and understanding became increasingly arduous during these instances. The question emerged: What can be relied upon when the script gets flipped, and memories of past conversations fade? How does one anchor oneself and build a foundation that endures the test of time? It became a quest for something steadfast and resilient in the face of forgetfulness.

My spouse is challenged with the concept of resilience and consistency—qualities that can withstand the fluctuations of memory and the adversities posed by the unpredictable nature of life. I know with consistent treatment; in creating lasting connections, he will discover the core principles that transcend the ephemeral nature of forgetfulness.

Seeking respect becomes a challenging task when one believes they already offer it, only to realize they fall short in certain aspects.

Likewise, the difficulty intensifies when love isn't reciprocated in the manner one requires due to personal struggles. This dynamic creates a complex and tangled web of emotions, resulting in a situation that feels profoundly disordered. It's like living on two different planets. In the face of dilemmas, a pressing question emerges: What steps can one take to navigate and unravel this complicated mesh?

Dealing with this situation means tackling it from different angles. First up, you got to do some serious self-reflection. Take a good, honest look at what you've been doing and admit where you could do better in showing respect. Once you're aware of these things, you're all set to make positive changes and build more genuine relationships.

Contemplating the wisdom found in Proverbs 18:24 says, "A man that hath friends must shew himself friendly: and there is a friend that sticketh closer than a brother." To have good friends, you need to be friendly and show kindness. Friendships require effort and care. The second part of the verse highlights that there can be a friend who is as loyal and close as family, possibly even more dependable than a sibling. It's a reminder that building and keeping friendships involves being supportive, approachable, and kind to others. This is something we should all strive to do in our lives, as it helps create a better, more compassionate world for everyone.

Let's replace the word friends with love. To have love, one must exhibit qualities of love. To experience and receive love, it is essential to embody, and express qualities associated with love. This sentiment underscores the reciprocity inherent in the concept of love, suggesting that genuine and meaningful connections are forged when individuals actively cultivate attributes such as kindness, compassion, understanding, and empathy.

Simultaneously, understanding the root causes of the obstacles in receiving love becomes imperative. Identifying personal issues hindering the reception of love is a courageous step towards self-discovery. This acknowledgment allows for targeted efforts in addressing and reducing these obstacles, cultivating a more conducive environment for love to flourish.

Also, communication plays a key role in untangling this difficult situation. Open and honest conversations about expectations, feelings, and the challenges each party faces can pave the way for mutual understanding. Sharing vulnerabilities and expressing needs sets the stage for sustaining a healthier and more balanced dynamic.

Chapter 5 - Emotional Turmoil

Being married to a Vietnam veteran who wrestles with PTSD and ADHD and lost his photographic memory and precise time management unfolds as a complexified emotional rollercoaster ride, characterized by a multitude of feelings and challenges that both partners must navigate.

I felt a profound sense of pride in his service to our country. In a way, I envisioned our union as a tribute to his commitment and sacrifices during a pivotal chapter in history. I admired the strength and endurance that he must have developed through the challenges he faced during his service, and it deepened my respect and admiration for him.

As I mentioned earlier, after marriage and a week's honeymoon, we had 5 people living at our home. My emotional journey consists of seeing my spouse with a steep descent into periods of intense anxiety, hypervigilance, and mood swings. The surprised approaches of communication, flashbacks, and nightmares transported him back to the traumas of war, evoking a sense of helplessness and I am wondering what on earth have I gotten myself into.

When we were able to travel or get some time alone, there were moments of connection and understanding that illuminated the strength and hope inherent in the relationship.

Shared experiences and enduring support become sources of peace and comfort. These highs, however, are compared with lows where the invisible wounds of war made their presence known.

As we started our journey together, I felt proud to be with someone who had devoted part of his life to serving a cause bigger than himself. The sacrifices he made during the war, the bonds he formed in difficult times, and his experiences as a Vietnam veteran became a key part of who he is—the person I chose to spend my life with.

Our age difference of 9 years was envisioned as a dynamic aspect of our relationship, intended to bring forth a harmonious blend of wisdom, maturity, vitality, love, and security. The notion behind this age gap was rooted in the belief that the varied experiences and perspectives accumulated over the additional years would contribute to the richness and depth of our connection. It would bring a wealth of wisdom, garnered from navigating the complexities of life and learning valuable lessons along the way. This wisdom, in turn, was anticipated to serve as a source of guidance and insight, bringing together a supportive and enlightened partnership.

Maturity, an intrinsic quality associated with the passage of time, was seen as a stabilizing force in our relationship. The hope was that this age difference would facilitate a balanced interplay of perspectives, with both partners contributing their unique insights to create a well-rounded and emotionally mature connection. About which he and I were so hopeful.

Vitality, emanating from the partner with a younger age, was anticipated to infuse our relationship with energy, enthusiasm, and a zest for life. This injection of vitality aimed to complement the stability brought by the more seasoned partner, creating a dynamic and vibrant partnership.

Love, the cornerstone of any meaningful relationship, was expected to transcend age, deepening with shared experiences, mutual understanding, and the passage of time. The foundation of our connection rested on the conviction that love has the capacity to mature and evolve over the years. This belief was integral to our relationship, providing a cornerstone of reassurance. Particularly when reflecting on the depth of love I had invested in my first marriage, where my heart was so fully engaged, the need for a safe and secure haven became paramount.

Not knowing the degree of being married to a Vietnam veteran with PTSD and ADHD entails a complexity of understanding, empathy, and endurance. It is a journey that simultaneously embraces the profound beauty of love and connection and obstacles with the challenging realities of navigating the impact of war-related trauma and attention difficulties on the relationship. Honestly, I am not there yet.

Entering into my second marriage with a sense of healing, I carried with me the residue of past wounds. Although I approached the union with a mended spirit, the scars from previous experiences lingered. This realization prompted me to tread cautiously, mindful of the vulnerabilities that came with the journey of devotion.

In the face of the complexities brought by past relationships, I sought a sanctuary within our connection—a place where compassion could not only endure but also evolve, offering peace and understanding as we navigated through emotions and shared experiences.

I believed security, both emotional and practical, was considered an essential outcome of the age difference. The idea was that the partner with more years would provide a sense of security through their life experiences, stability, and a nurturing presence, cultivating an environment where both partners could feel safe and supported.

However, as we uncovered the complexities of life as a married couple, I began to realize the depth of the challenges that accompany being married to a Vietnam veteran. The impact of war on his mental and emotional well-being became more apparent, and I discovered the complexities that PTSD and other experiences had introduced into our relationship.

I became shocked, horrified, scared, so angry, and upset that another marriage I entered into seemed to echo hauntingly familiar patterns.

The initial optimism that accompanies the beginning of a marital journey was overshadowed by a disconcerting sense of déjà vu as if I were confronted with echoes of past challenges that had left indelible marks on my emotional landscape.

The horror stemmed from the realization that certain dynamics, reminiscent of previous experiences, were resurfacing. The specter of unresolved issues and unaddressed concerns cast a shadow over the existing union, triggering an unsettling wave of fear and apprehension. The prospect of navigating through similar challenges evoked a sense of vulnerability as if history were threatening to repeat itself.

Anger surged within me, fueled by the frustration of finding myself in a situation that mirrored past tribulations. The recognition that I was facing familiar struggles triggered a visceral response. It was directed not only at external circumstances but also at the internal struggle with a situation that seemed all too familiar yet equally distressing.

Scared and upset, I found myself struggling with a mix of emotions that intensified the complexity of the situation. The fear stemmed from the uncertainty of whether the marriage would follow a different trajectory or succumb to the challenges that had plagued previous relationships. Upset by the apparent recurrence of patterns, I questioned my own choices and decisions, wondering how I had found myself traversing familiar emotional territory once again.

For several years, I found myself navigating through a tumultuous journey, having uncertainty and not knowing where to turn for guidance. Despite seeking counseling, studying my Bible, and immersing myself in literature rooted in faith to aid in my struggles, the challenges persisted. The proverb "It takes two to tangle" echoed in my mind, emphasizing the shared responsibility in a relationship.

As I recounted earlier, the individuals I sought support were either disinterested or interpreted my expressions in a way that diminished the complexities I faced with the man they knew. Living with him brought forth a different reality, one laden with baggage that cast a shadow over the idyllic image they held. I thought I wasn't the one suited for him—a woman capable of embracing love, kindness, and understanding, envisioning dreams that could harmoniously unfold with her husband.

The weight of emotional turmoil consumed me. Despite our conversations before and during marriage, the reality starkly contrasted with my expectations. The disparity left me questioning the nature of my being, leading to sleepless nights, emotional exhaustion, and a physical toll reflected in a weight gain of over 30 lbs. The sense of not being loved the way I should be loved permeated me, transforming my outward appearance and affecting my sense of self.

In the midst of this emotional maelstrom, I am struggling with the paradox of having a man in my life who says he loves me, despite occasional glimpses of the person I once dated, existing in his own world.

Navigating through daily life with him became a constant juggling act, as I tried to remember his specific preferences and instructions, often reiterated repeatedly. The routine was punctuated by his detailed directives on how things should be done, creating an environment where adherence to his expectations felt like a relentless task.

The aftermath of disagreements unfolded as a barrage of critiques, either conveyed directly or through text messages, labeling me with various derogatory terms.

The emotional toll of this recurrent cycle was overwhelming, constituting a form of emotional abuse that stirred haunting echoes of my experiences in my first marriage. In my current marriage, the weight of his persistent demands, yelling loudly and the subsequent verbal assaults took a toll on my emotional well-being. His face would be horrifying to me. Is there a man that could love me?

In the realm of our daily interactions, I found myself walking on a precarious tightrope, attempting to meet his expectations while dealing with the emotional aftermath of our clashes.

The cyclical nature of this dynamic created an environment fraught with tension, uncertainty, and a pervasive sense of inadequacy.

The relentless reminders of how I fell short of his expectations, coupled with the emotional strain, became a daunting backdrop to our daily lives. It was a scenario where the minutiae of daily tasks became entangled with a web of emotional complexities, creating a space where the boundaries between personal preferences and emotional well-being were blurred.

I had no idea, this journey was not for the weak but a profound odyssey for those fortified with strength, courage, and unwavering commitment. It demands a tenacity that withstands the storms of emotional turbulence, and the relentless challenges posed by the aftermath of war. It beckons individuals who possess an indomitable spirit, capable of navigating the intricate maze of emotions, uncertainties, and involvements in being intimately connected with a Vietnam veteran.

As I began to learn, this journey is for those who understand that strength is not just a physical attribute but a reservoir of emotional fortitude, a reservoir that must be tapped into during moments of darkness and uncertainty.

It calls for hearts that can endure the weight of witnessing a loved one who struggles with the enduring impact of war, hearts that remain steadfast when faced with the unpredictable nature of PTSD and ADHD.

Would I be able to embrace a journey to find peace in the midst of chaos? Or would I be able to cultivate patience when faced with the uncharted territory of communication challenges, and who could adapt with grace to the ever-evolving dynamics within a relationship marked by war-related trauma? This expedition demands a commitment to mutual understanding, open communication, and the perpetual pursuit of resilience. Was this me?

To put this simply, this journey is a call to arms for those equipped not only with unconditional love but with an unyielding commitment to weathering the highs and lows. I would have to become some type of soldier for this!

The journey became not only about honoring his service but also about navigating the realities of the lingering effects of war on our everyday lives. It required a recalibration of expectations, an embrace of patience, and a commitment to supporting each other through the unique challenges that emerged.

Being married to a Vietnam veteran was not just about pride; it was a commitment to a journey that demanded empathy, strength, and an unwavering dedication to forming a relationship that could withstand the complexities of war's aftermath. Was I up to the task?

Chapter 6 - Decision Time

In my frequent contemplation of whether to confront or end my almost 15-year marriage with a spouse who has not consistently pursued therapy for PTSD and ADHD, I find myself immersed in a complex and emotionally charged process that demands careful consideration of various factors.

On my journey, I have deepened my understanding of PTSD and ADHD. I have recognized the unique challenges these conditions pose for my unexpected stranger and the impact they may have on the dynamics of the relationship. I have educated myself about the symptoms, triggers, and potential coping mechanisms associated with each condition.

As I contemplate my own emotional well-being within the confines of the relationship, the journey has been arduous and challenging, reaching a point where I doubted my ability to endure. The breaking point became glaringly evident last year when I found myself collapsing in the emergency room.

Faced with a dire situation, I urgently called upon my spouse to transport me to the ER since I was in no condition to drive. However, he seemed to lose track of time, displaying a lack of readiness to take immediate action. The urgency of the situation didn't register with him.

Our journey to the ER was marked by heated arguments, and my physical condition worsened. Experiencing excruciating headaches, I felt as if my head was on the verge of exploding. Upon arriving at the ER and going through the check-in process, the culmination of stress and illness reached its peak, and I collapsed. Swift action was taken, and medical tests were conducted during my three-day hospital stay. Despite all the examinations, everything appeared normal, leaving doctors and nurses puzzled as to the root cause of my debilitating headaches.

During this challenging time, my unexpected stranger attempted to spend the night at the hospital, unaware that what I truly needed was a break from his presence. In reality, he needed to be at home, offering support to my mom.

He believed that reading a particular book could provide the solution to what I was experiencing. However, he lacked a true understanding of the depth and complexity of my struggles. It was beyond his comprehension to grasp the challenges I was facing. Was the book working for him? Recognizing the gravity of my situation, one of my caring sisters, who was well aware of my circumstances, intervened. She called me to relay to him to return home to allow me some much-needed rest. This way, he could also be there for my mom, who was left alone at our residence.

As I lay in the hospital bed, contemplating the trajectory of my life and its poignant turns, the doctor entered my room with a genuine inquiry about the circumstances surrounding my emotional state. Overwhelmed with a surge of emotions, tears welled up as I began recounting the complex journey of my recent years.

I shared the story of my commitment to caring for my parents, a journey that had led me out of state for several years. Our family had undergone a significant relocation, hastily moving to a new home that could accommodate not only my husband and me but also my aging parents. The details unfolded like a whirlwind – the swift transition, the retrieval of my parents from another state, and the process of settling them into our new home.

Amidst the vivid memories, the narrative shifted to the shared holidays with our entire family and friends, marred by an unfortunate wave of illness that affected us all.

Yet, the focus turned somber as I narrated the decline of my beloved father's health. As his daughter and power of attorney, my days were consumed with constant communication with medical professionals, orchestrating his care from afar. The weight of his illness kept me from being with him in person for weeks, but our conversations continued, bridging the distance. During this difficult time, I deeply appreciated the help of my husband, who stepped in to assist with my dad's care, offering support when I needed it most.

Despite valiant efforts, my father's health continued to falter, and after an arduous two months marked by hospital visits, he eventually passed away. The loss reverberated through our family, echoing the shattered pieces of my heart. I was Daddy's little girl, the one who shared deep conversations with him, and reciprocally, the one who cared for him as he had cared for his wife and sons. After the hospital called, my two cousins and I went to see Dad lifeless. I sat by him, holding his warm hand in the hospital room, only to feel the gradual chill as he departed this world.

In the hospital's quiet corridors, I wept beside him, uttering words of love and farewell. "Oh Daddy, we love you dearly, and your absence leaves an irreplaceable void. We find solace in the hope of being reunited with you, knowing that the first face you'll see is that of Jesus." With a heavy heart, I left the hospital, knowing that my father would not return home again.

The grief, the wake, the funeral, the handling of his estate, and making sure my mom was taken care of had me going nonstop. I cried many nights as I heard my mother cry. She often called me by her husband's name, but I understood. I was proud to know I looked like him and his mother. And that was her husband for almost 66 years. My husband didn't understand the debts of Dad's and my relationship. Helping him to cope with his problems meant I was a caregiver to not only my parents but to him too.

Of course, I gave the doctor the short version, but he told me I was experiencing tension headaches. I hadn't heard of them I heard of migraines. I was stressed with muscle tension, and throbbing headaches affecting both sides of the head, face, and neck. And I couldn't sleep at night.

As my spouse's work hours diminished, leaving him without the capacity for full-time employment and consequently without insurance coverage for me, the situation became precarious. While his veteran status ensured his continuous coverage, I found myself without that safety net. Upon securing federal health insurance, a turning point emerged. My spouse could engage in temporary employment through agencies, and I, in turn, gained access to my own medical and dental coverage.

The resilience I summoned within myself, urging my body to persevere through the challenges I had faced, played a pivotal role. It was during this period that, despite my internal encouragement, the strain on my well-being reached a critical juncture, leading to my collapse during the ER check-in.

The subsequent months unfolded with a series of doctor's visits and appointments with specialists. Recognizing the need for comprehensive support, I received recommendations to connect with individuals who would steadfastly stand by me, regardless of the circumstances. Additionally, the guidance included reaching out to a psychiatrist and therapist and acknowledging the importance of mental health care in navigating the complexities of the situation.

Now, I can see how the challenges affected my mental health, emotional resilience, and overall happiness. I had to acknowledge my own needs and whether they aligned with the current state of this relationship.

Determined not to succumb to the prevailing circumstances, I observed my spouse moving through life seemingly unaffected, while I felt at my wit's end. No more, I thought; change was imperative! Committing to taking charge of my life with the guidance of God, I recognized that I couldn't control others, nor did I aspire to. Taking the initiative, I reached out to my circle of close girlfriends, who, with unfiltered candor and encouragement, provided the reality check I needed.

Empowered by their support, I took the step of scheduling an appointment with a psychiatrist, who, in turn, connected me with a therapist. Together, they became instrumental in helping me establish clear and healthy boundaries that prioritized my emotional and mental well-being, emphasizing the importance of self-care. Additionally, I found solace and understanding in a support network for caregivers, propelling me forward on a path of positive transformation. With this newfound support and determination, I felt I was on my way to reclaiming control over my life.

In the subsequent phase of my journey, I turned to gratitude, expressing heartfelt thanks to God for the guidance required to set myself on the right path. Acknowledging the need for a sanctuary within my own space, I endeavored to create an environment conducive to thoughtful examination, meditation, and the establishment of new, nourishing routines. However, this endeavor proved to be a challenge for my husband, who struggled to comprehend the significance of these changes.

With a foundation laid for personal growth, the time had come for transparent and sincere communication with significant individuals in my life. Engaging in open dialogues with my mother, brothers, son, and spouse, I fearlessly expressed my thoughts, emotions, and concerns, cultivating an atmosphere devoid of judgment. These conversations marked a pivotal moment in reshaping the dynamics of my relationships.

Recognizing the weightiness of decisions made during this transformative journey, I intentionally allowed myself periods of deep reflection. Understanding that choices of such magnitude require patience and thoughtful consideration, I provided the essential space to assess the ever-evolving landscape of my feelings, thoughts, and the intricate dynamics of the relationship over time. This approach became a cornerstone in navigating the complexities of my personal and relational evolution.

As I progress along my journey, I am embracing the art of living my dream life in the present. Some may question how one can embark on such a path after enduring significant challenges, but I respond with a resounding "Why not!" Why dwell on what I may lack or the uncertainties that lie beyond my reach? Instead, I choose to channel my focus into thoughts of thankfulness, gratefulness, hopefulness, faith, and trust in a benevolent God who possesses an intimate understanding of me, surpassing my own self-awareness. His boundless love is evident in the sacrificial gift of His Son, who bore the weight of my sins, granting me the promise of eternal life.

Confronted with the choice between the low road and the high road, I wholeheartedly opt for the latter. This decision is rooted in the belief that gratitude, hope, faith, and trust pave the way for a richer and more meaningful journey.

By focusing on the positive aspects of life and embracing the divine love that surrounds me, I navigate the high road, mastering a mindset that leads to enduring fulfillment and spiritual abundance.

Chapter 7 - The Aftermath

Illustrating the consequences of my decision holds significance. I've chosen to let God transform me while entrusting the care of my unforeseen life companion to Him. While articulating this decision is straightforward, the actual implementation poses challenges, yet it remains entirely achievable.

I found myself burdened with stress, tension, and negative thoughts, feeling weighed down by the challenges I faced. I was challenged with both his PTSD and the behaviors that dominate our interactions. It's a delicate balance to emphasize and be sensitive when faced with treatment that feels challenging. Our relationship deviates from what is considered normal, a stark contrast to the harmonious partnership my parents shared, marked by collaboration and love throughout their nearly 66-year marriage. The stark contrast leaves my head spinning, as this is a situation I never envisioned for myself and one I didn't actively choose.

Remaining with a man who struggles with mental illness comes with its set of advantages and disadvantages. Firstly, acknowledging his mental health challenges and recognizing the need for treatment is a positive step. Secondly, he's gradually gaining self-awareness, and understanding positively impacted our marriage. Thirdly, he's making efforts in his way, actively scheduling appointments, and seeking improvement.

Lastly, being aware of his strengths and weaknesses, particularly as he ages, implies a deeper involvement in his life, considering the significant 9-year age gap between us.

Reflecting on the fact that my unexpected charismatic companion hasn't undergone extensive treatment brings the realization that the journey toward becoming the man he envisions and the partner I require might be a prolonged one, spanning years. Faced with this understanding, the question that arises is: What steps do I take moving forward?

Embarking on a new endeavor often brings forth a cascade of aspirations and dreams, spanning from the immediate present to the foreseeable future. Within this venture, there exist both individual goals and shared aspirations between partners. The shared journey with a spouse amplifies the collective desire to engage in numerous activities and accomplishments together.

Reflecting on the wedding vows echoing in my ears—particularly the commitment to endure sickness and health—I recall being aware of certain challenges my spouse shared before our marriage. However, the discovery of additional problems blindsided both of us. It's a reminder that not everything about your spouse is revealed before marriage; some aspects unfold on the journey.

Hearing about successful marriages underscores the common theme of significant struggles. These couples acknowledge moments when packing up seemed like the only option, some did leave and return, while others chose to divorce and a new beginning. The complexities of marriage, with its twists and turns, are a shared experience among those who navigate the challenging path of commitment.

Achieving a happy marriage requires a foundation built on effective communication, mutual respect, and emotional support. Both partners need to be committed to understanding each other's needs, navigating challenges together, and continuously investing in the relationship. Flexibility, compromise, and the ability to forgive are essential, fostering an environment where growth and change are embraced. Shared values, common goals, and a sense of partnership contribute to a strong bond. Regular expressions of love, gratitude, and affection sustain the emotional connection. Moreover, maintaining individual identities and interests allows for personal growth within the context of the marriage. A happy marriage is an ongoing journey that thrives on nurturing the connection, weathering life's storms as a team, and finding joy in shared moments.

As we struggled with the recurrent challenges, we embarked on a shared exploration of the profound roots that could anchor our relationship. It is an ongoing process of refining our communication, deepening our appreciation, and cultivating a profound understanding that transcends the transient lapses. I pray that we aspire to build a foundation strong enough to withstand the unpredictable twists in life and embrace a journey marked by enduring connection and mutual growth.

The pivotal moment came during my hospital stay, prompting a necessary shift in focus toward my own well-being. It's often said that caregivers are prone to neglecting their own needs, prioritizing others' welfare. Recognizing this pattern, I understood the importance of establishing boundaries. It reminded me of the safety instructions on an airplane, emphasizing the need to secure one's mask before assisting others. Applying this principle in my life, I began to prioritize self-care, drawing strength from my deepening belief in God's Word. Through prayer and the practical application of newfound knowledge, I embarked on a transformative journey, emerging as a rejuvenated and empowered woman.

Surrendering this situation to God has been instrumental in fostering my personal growth and resilience. A true blessing came in the form of my therapist, whose kindness and attentive ear provided a safe space for my frustrations, hurt, and pain, without judgment. She once mentioned that it took about three months before she saw me smile— wow, I hadn't even realized. In moments of intense despair, when leaving seemed like the only option, her support became a lifeline.

Despite contemplating this decision multiple times, the weight of responsibility toward my mother and my spouse compels me to persevere. The realization that even a beautiful home loses its luster without genuine happiness pushes me to navigate these challenges, knowing others look to me for guidance and support.

I find gratitude in my unexpected stranger who became an integral part of my family. Despite the twists and turns of life, I deeply appreciate the unwavering dedication and effort he invests in supporting our family in his own way. His commitment to hard work is now evident, and he excels in his professional endeavors.

Each person's journey is unique, and mine is distinctly my own. Embracing the imperative of finding goodness in others, even if it's slender, I make a conscious effort to offer encouraging words and let them know they're in my prayers. I prayed for a transformation in myself, seeking to replace the anger, resentment, and frustration within me with love and kindness.

My unexpected and charming spouse is an individual with inherent qualities, and there's a limit to the expectations one can place on what lies ahead. Embracing my own identity is crucial on this distinctive journey through life. Although it may not align with what I initially desired, it is the reality I find myself in. Recognizing that there's a purpose for my presence, I acknowledge that life comes with its inherent challenges, yet I trust that God wouldn't assign me a task beyond my capacity to endure.

I read, do not underestimate yourself. Never think there's anything in this world you're not good enough for. A man is blessed to have you, or anyone is blessed to have you. I began to know I was happy again, enough, worthy, beautiful, smart, blessed, and thankful so I lived it.

I am loving, generous, a go-getter who loves to travel, appreciates organization, values punctuality, educated, entrepreneur, caregiver to two family members, and derives immense joy from accomplishing goals. My interests extend to singing, cooking, and nurturing my spiritual connection with the Lord. Making others happy brings me fulfillment, within the bounds of reason and understanding.

Becoming a pillar of support for a Vietnam veteran is an achievement in itself. Being the spouse of someone who served in a war, a warrior who not only fought physically but is now battling mental aftereffects, has brought me immense gratitude.

While not without its trials, this journey forges bonds of unparalleled strength. It is for those who believe in the transformative power of love and are willing to walk hand in hand through the valleys and peaks, navigating the complexities with a courage that defines the very essence of the human spirit.

The concept of love presents a challenge for me. I find solace in the love of God, my family, and my close friends, as they form the roots that have contributed to shaping who I am today. Some call it a "village". However, when it comes to my husband, the dynamics are on a different level. The emotional roller coaster becomes overwhelming, prompting me to adopt a more pragmatic approach, veering towards friendship or roommate dynamics. Accepting this reality, I strive to cultivate an atmosphere of peace, kindness and love within our home, doing what I can to promote harmony.

Amid the challenges, God is strengthening my resolve and wisdom, providing me with the patience to endure while maintaining my sense of self. It's essential to advocate for myself, set clear boundaries, prioritize my well-being, and nurture self-love in order to extend that capacity to others. Seeking God, and professional support, along with the encouragement of family and close friends, plays a vital role in this empowering journey.

Chapter 8 - Conclusion

As I reflect on my marriage to a Vietnam veteran coping with PTSD and ADHD it is a unique journey layered with obstacles and profound lessons. One crucial lesson is the significance of empathy and understanding. Living with a partner dealing with these conditions requires a deep well of compassion. It requires recognizing the impact of traumatic experiences on their mental health and understanding the manifestations of their conditions that might affect daily life.

Communication emerges as another pivotal lesson. Open and honest dialogue becomes essential in navigating the complexities of living with a spouse dealing with mental illness. It involves establishing an environment where both partners feel comfortable expressing their feelings, concerns, and needs. Effective communication becomes a cornerstone in building mutual support and strengthening the bond amidst the challenges.

Patience is a virtue that takes center stage in this journey. Dealing with the manifestations of his conditions often requires a considerable amount of understanding. Knowing that the healing process is gradual and may involve setbacks is crucial. Patience becomes a tool for both partners to navigate through difficult moments, along with resilience and perseverance.

Caring for a partner with mental health challenges demands a lot of emotional energy. Learning to prioritize self-care is crucial for maintaining one's own well-being. It involves setting boundaries, seeking personal support, and taking the necessary steps to recharge emotionally. This is a challenge for me, but I am learning along the way.

Learning to be flexible in plans and adaptable to changing circumstances becomes a valuable skill. It involves embracing the fluidity of life and being prepared to navigate unexpected challenges with resilience.

Finally, this journey teaches the strength of love and commitment. Despite the hurdles posed by mental health conditions, a marriage can endure and flourish with unwavering love and commitment. It involves recognizing the humanity in one another, acknowledging imperfections, and choosing to stand together through the ups and downs.

In essence, being in this type of union unfolds as a profound learning experience, encompassing lessons in empathy, communication, patience, self-care, flexibility, and the enduring power of compassion and commitment.

Acknowledging that I am still in the process of growth, I am conflicted about the ongoing journey to become the wife of my unexpected stranger needs, even as I confront the reality that my own needs may not always be met in the way I envision. This continuous learning experience requires a daily commitment to maintaining focus on myself before extending that attention to others.

The journey unfolds as a conscious effort to cultivate self-awareness and prioritize personal well-being. Each day becomes an opportunity for introspection, understanding my own desires, and acknowledging the areas that require attention and nurturing. It's about recognizing that my growth as an individual directly impacts the dynamics of the relationship.

Navigating the complexities of meeting my partner's needs while balancing my own becomes a delicate dance. The commitment to self-focus isn't a neglect of the relationship but rather an essential step in ensuring that I approach it from a place of strength and authenticity. It involves setting those boundaries, communicating openly about expectations, and understanding that self-care is not selfish but a prerequisite for sustaining a healthy partnership.

This commitment extends beyond the superficial layers of daily routines and reaches into the depths of emotional strength. It involves acknowledging that my journey is ongoing, and perfection is not the goal. Instead, the focus is on continuous improvement and self-discovery. The journey becomes a daily practice of mindfulness, where I intentionally carve out moments for self-reflection, self-care, and personal pursuits.

In essence, admitting that I am not there yet is not a declaration of failure but an acknowledgment of the ongoing evolution as an individual and a partner.

To you, my esteemed reader, the notion of closure serves as more than just a finality; it encapsulates a profound sense of completion and understanding. It is not merely the end of a chapter but a gateway to a new beginning, a moment where loose ends find their resolution and emotions find their equilibrium. In exploring the concept of closure, we probe into the complex web of emotions, where acceptance intertwines with reflection, providing a sense of peace that paves the way for healing and growth. This journey toward closure is not a linear path but a dynamic process, as we navigate through the puzzle of experiences, acknowledging the complexities of letting go and embracing the transformative power of closure in forging a path forward.

I trust that this book has served as a source of inspiration for those facing similar challenges. Opening up and sharing my story has been a cathartic experience, driven by the belief that personal narratives can resonate with others navigating comparable journeys. The decision to pen down my experiences was not only prompted by external suggestions but also by the guidance of my therapist, who recognized the therapeutic value of such an endeavor.

Through the pages of this book, I've unraveled the threads of my life, unraveling the choices and actions that have shaped my journey. It's more than just a recounting of events; it's a courageous confrontation of fears, a patient exploration of self, and a transformative process that has fortified my resilience.

Engaging in writing has evolved into a profound tool for self-inspection and soul-searching, allowing me to explore the intricate details of my own life. This process is not merely a mechanical exercise; rather, it is a deeply emotional journey. As I navigate through the realms of words and sentences, I unearth a myriad of emotions that accompany the exploration of my thoughts and experiences. Writing becomes a vessel for self-discovery, unveiling layers of feelings, memories, and reflections that might otherwise remain obscured. It is through the emotional nuances woven into the fabric of words that I find a richer understanding of myself and the elaborate weave of my life.

The motivation behind sharing my story extends beyond the personal realm; it's a gentle reminder to those who might be tempted to rush into new or older relationships without affording themselves the time for reflection and healing.

Relationships, both failed and successful, offer valuable lessons. Sometimes, the need for growth lies within us, and other times, it's a shared journey. Regardless, the essence lies in dedicating time to heal, reflect, and rediscover self-love.

Life, with all its shortness, carries a purpose for each of us. This realization has been a driving force, urging me to seize every moment with wisdom, infuse joy into my existence, and cherish the profound bonds of love. Divine guidance, professional assistance, and the constant support of family and friends have been instrumental in this transformative process.

As we move toward our individual paths, let us not squander the precious gift of time. Instead, let us approach life with a reservoir of knowledge, embracing joy, happiness, and love. Through mutual support and the understanding that each journey is unique, we can craft lives filled with purpose and fulfillment.

Chapter 9 - Final Thoughts

A few things I forgot to mention in this book. In the midst of seeking divine guidance for uniting with my unexpected stranger, memories of a dream during my engagement flooded my thoughts. In this ethereal vision, God adorned the heavens, the earth serving as His majestic backdrop. From the Divine realm, a resounding voice assures me to wed this stranger, promising that He would always be with me.

As I embarked on this unexpected marital journey, I struggled with uncertainty, questioning if I had accurately interpreted God's directive during our initial years together. Marriage, a complex embroidery, can either weave individuals together or unravel their connection over time. Unlike my previous marriage, where God offered an exit strategy, this union held a distinct purpose—lessons designed to sculpt my character.

In the embroidery of divine wisdom, I discerned that marrying this handsome gentleman was a divine orchestration. Through the obstacles and triumphs, I gradually comprehended God's purpose— transformative growth. His voice echoed in my consciousness, emphasizing that in the realm of marriage, personal evolution is inevitable.

God's counsel echoed in my ears, unveiling profound insights about love, particularly for those struggling with mental illness. It dawned on me that navigating such complexities required divine intervention. Thus, I embarked on a journey where only God's guidance could illuminate the path, to glue understanding and compassion amid the unique challenges we faced.

In the unfolding chapters of our marriage, I discovered that prayer, a mutual understanding with kindness, fortified by divine wisdom, can transcend the hurdles posed by mental illness. This revelation can fortify our bond but illuminate the profound truth that God's purpose in our union can extend beyond our individual growth— It will encompass a shared dedication, where we collectively commit to not only embracing but also deeply understanding one another, especially when faced with adversities and challenging circumstances.

In reflecting on the narrative of my life, I once imagined a hierarchy of love, with God at the top as my greatest source of affection, followed by my Dad as my second love, and then a unique love my spouse—the second unexpected stranger. My belief was that the love I received from God and my Dad should set a standard for how I expected to be treated by my husband, creating a distinct paradigm for our relationship.

The paradox prompts reflection on the intricacies of love and communication within the context of marriage. It raises questions about bridging the gap between expectations and reality, and how to navigate a situation where the idealized love portrayed by God and my Dad differs from the more complex dynamics within the realm of spousal affection.

And so, the narrative of my life presses on, unfolding its chapters and weaving layers of experiences that shape the ongoing saga. The journey, marked by twists and turns, remains a testament to strength and growth. As the pages turn, new characters enter the stage, and fresh struggles emerge, adding layers to the evolving tale.

As the story unfolds, my relationship with my unexpected stranger takes on new dimensions. Confronting unspoken fears and hidden insecurities that test our connection is particularly challenging when one struggles to stay on the same page or hasn't dealt with the past. It's interesting how one can communicate effortlessly with others, but when it comes to our conversations, he often struggles to express himself in a way that conveys love and understanding. Moments of joy are often intertwined with misunderstandings, moments of clarity, and instances of not being truly heard, revealing the complexities of our emotional journey.

We are two individuals, each carrying our own needs for love and understanding. Despite our shared desire for connection, the way we express and receive love sometimes feels out of sync, and that creates a distance between us. Instead of bridging the gap, it can often feel like we're speaking different languages, making it harder to connect on a deeper level.

As we maneuver these challenges, we hope to learn the importance of vulnerability and communication, realizing that love is not just about harmony but also about working through differences. Each revelation could deepen our bond, forcing us to reassess our individual identities within the partnership. How will we rise to meet these challenges, and what truths about ourselves and each other will emerge from this journey?

Amidst the unexpected turns and character developments, the story persists, a vivid mosaic of joy, sorrow, triumphs, and setbacks. It becomes a confirmation of the indomitable spirit that propels me forward, even when faced with the unknown. As I steer the uncharted territories of my narrative, the echoes of the past resonate, guiding my steps and influencing the choices that shape the chapters yet to be written.

As we continue on this journey, may we all remember that love, patience, and faith guide us through even the toughest moments.

Chapter 10 - Encouragement for Your Journey

As we navigate the winding paths of life, we often encounter challenges that test our strength and resilience. In these moments, it's vital to find sources of encouragement and inspiration to guide us forward.

This chapter is dedicated to uplifting verses from the Bible and motivational quotes that remind us of the hope, love, and strength that can be found in faith and community. May these words resonate with you, bringing comfort and encouragement as you continue your journey.

Psalm 121:1-2 (NIV): "I lift up my eyes to the mountains— where does my help come from? My help comes from the Lord, the Maker of heaven and earth."

Proverbs 12:4 (NIV): "A wife of noble character is her husband's crown, but a disgraceful wife is like decay in his bones."

Ephesians 5:25 (NIV): "Husbands, love your wives, just as Christ loved the church and gave himself up for her."

Ephesians 5:33 (NIV): "However, each one of you also must love his wife as he loves himself, and the wife must respect her husband."

1 Peter 3:1-2 (NIV): "Wives, in the same way, submit (yield) yourselves to your own husbands so that, if any of them do not believe the word, they may be won over without words by the behavior of their wives, when they see the purity and reverence of your lives."

1 Corinthians 13:4-7 (NIV): "Love is patient, love is kind. It does not envy, it does not boast, it is not proud. It does not dishonor others, it is not self-seeking, it is not easily angered, and it keeps no record of wrongs. Love does not delight in evil but rejoices with the truth. It always protects, always trusts, always hopes, always perseveres."

"To truly know and love your spouse, you must first embark on the journey of self-discovery. As you understand yourself, you open the door to understanding and appreciating your partner."

"A strong relationship is built on communication, trust, and understanding. Face challenges with open hearts and minds, and let your love be the guiding light."

"In the sanctuary of marriage, self-discovery is the sacred journey that leads to deeper connections. Embrace the process, and you'll find that understanding yourself is the key to understanding your spouse."

"Love is not just a feeling; it's a choice. Choose to love each other every day, even on the tough days. Your commitment will sustain and strengthen your bond."

"In the dance of a relationship, remember that you're partners, not competitors. Work together, communicate openly, and dance through life with grace and understanding."

In closing, I heard a speaker say we are to write our own story. My narrative endures as an ever-evolving chronicle that unfolds with each passing moment, offering a glimpse into the profound artwork of a life in perpetual motion. This journey, far from reaching its end, continues to weave its threads through time, inviting anticipation for the unwritten chapters that lie ahead.

How will you embrace the unwritten chapters of your life?

www.ingramcontent.com/pod-product-compliance
Lightning Source LLC
Chambersburg PA
CBHW060132260626
47160CB00005B/2082